For the Catchpoles - Eoin
For little monsters everywhere - Robert

First published in the United Kingdom in 2020 by
Pavilion Children's Books
43 Great Ormond Street
London
WC1N 3HZ

An imprint of Pavilion Books Limited.

Publisher: Neil Dunnicliffe
Editor: Hattie Grylls
Designer: Sarah Crookes

Text © Eoin McLaughlin 2020
Illustrations © Robert Starling 2020

The moral rights of the author and illustrator have been asserted

ISBN: 9781843654384

A CIP catalogue record for this book is available from the British Library.

10 9 8 7 6 5 4 3 2 1

Reproduction by Mission, Hong Kong
Printed by Toppan Leefung Ltd., China

This book can be ordered directly from the publisher online at
www.pavilionbooks.com, or try your local bookshop.

Stop! If you plan to sleep tonight,
then DON'T turn the page...
just there, on the right.

THIS BOOK IS NOT A BEDTIME STORY!

Eoin McLaughlin
Robert Starling

This book is NOT
a bedtime story.

It's scary, strange
and rather gory.

Bedtime stories
make you sleepy.
This book won't.
It's much too CREEPY.

This book stars me –
the World's Scariest Monster!

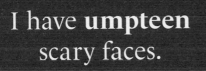

I have **umpteen** scary faces.

And I can scare *you* with a single…

...BOO!

My middle
name is 'Terror'.

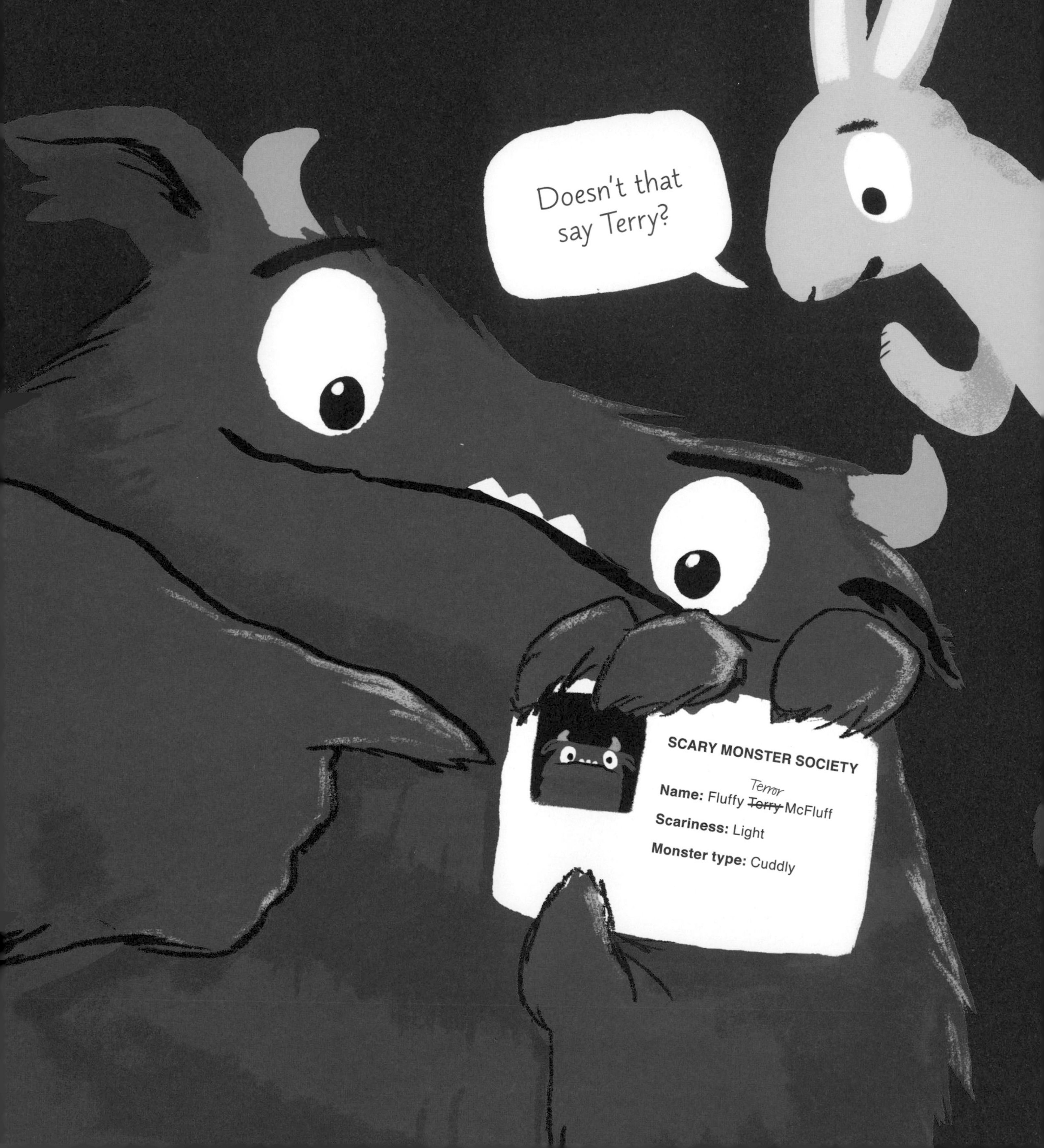

Look at my teeth!
Look at my claws!

Listen to my
great big roars!

SILENCE!

Now pay attention. The story is starting…

Ahem.

My monster gang
are a horrible bunch
They'll spread you on toast
and have you for lunch.

This lonely wood
is where we brew
our dark and filthy
monster stew.

Could do with a little more tarragon, but otherwise, it's scrumptious.
Oh that's so kind! It's my mother's recipe.

Now we're in a haunted house.
We'll spook that ghost
and scare that mouse.

Isn't that Bobby
wearing a sheet?

ARRRRRR!

You're in our ghastly grip,
sailing on our ghostly ship!

I feel a bit sick.

Me too.

Is that a shark?!
That really
IS scary!

What's more scary
than a shark?
I'll show you!
It's the darkest…

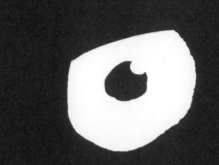

Aha! We're in
a creepy cave.
Let's snarl at bats
and misbehave.

We are really, truly, vastly, super-duper

MEGA-GHASTLY!

What's that you say?
You're still not scared?
There's one last fright
that we've prepared.

ZZZZZZ

This book was not
a bedtime story.
It was scary, strange…
and rather… yaaaawwwny.

I don't need tucking in!

I'm a raving beast.
You heard me roar.
I'm too scary for sleep...

Snore, snore, snore.